Presented to

_____

by_____

on_____

I'm Kaitlyn!

I HAVE IMPORTANT JOBS TO DO

Crystal Bowman
Illustrated by Elena Kucharik

Tyndale House Publishers, Inc.
WHEATON, ILLINOIS

Visit Tyndale's exciting Web site at www.tyndale.com

Edited by Betty Free Swanberg
Designed by Catherine Bergstrom

Library of Congress Cataloging-in-Publication Data
Bowman, Crystal.
    I'm Kaitlyn!: I have important jobs to do / Crystal Bowman ; illustrated by Elena Kucharik.
       p. cm. — (Little blessings)
Summary: In rhyming text, Kaitlyn tells about all the things she does around the house,
including taking care of her kitty and reading Bible stories by herself.
    ISBN 0-8423-7671-2 (alk. paper)
    1. Helping behavior—Religious aspects—Christianity—Juvenile literature. 2. Christian life—
Juvenile literature. [1. Helpfulness. 2. Christian life.] I. Kucharik, Elena, ill. II. Title. III. Little
blessings picture books.
    BV4647.H4 B69 2003
    242'.62—dc21   2002015172

Printed in Italy

09 08 07 06 05 04
7 6 5 4 3 2

To Ann and Linda:
Thanks for being a blessing in my life.

Work with enthusiasm, as though
you were working for the Lord
rather than for people.
EPHESIANS 6:7

My name's Kaitlyn,
and I pray,
"Thank you for
a brand new day.
Bless me, Lord,
for I need you.
I have *important
things to do.*"

Tuck in the blankets
   on my bed,
Fluff the pillow
   for my head.

Pick my clothes up
off the floor,
Put them where
they were before.

Time to feed
  my kitty cat
Curled up on
  her kitty mat.
"Here's your food
  and water too"—
All these *important*
  things to do.

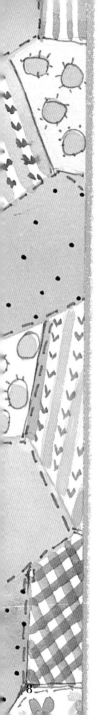

I can help
   when I am told,
"Kaitlyn, here
   are socks to fold."
Red socks, blue socks,
   green and white.
Which is left
   and which is right?

9

Make a snack
   to share at noon.
Friends will be here
   very soon—

Parker, Jack,
and Zoë too—
All these *important*
things to do.

Sun is shining—
   go outside.
Let's take Kitty
   for a ride.
Careful now,
   we'll start out slow.
Faster, faster,
   here we go!

"Kaitlyn, push me
   in the swing!"
Swinging high,
   we laugh and sing.
"Lord, you made
   the sky so blue.
Thanks for *important
   things to do.*"

Red and yellow,
   green and pink,
Thirsty flowers
   need a drink.

Sprinkle with
  a garden hose.
Uh-oh! Watch out
  for your toes!

Party time
   for friends and me.
Wash the teacups
   after tea.
"Kaitlyn, can you
   tie my shoe?"
These are *important*
   things to do.

Find my Bible
  on the shelf,
Read the stories
  by myself.
"Lord, you said
  some mighty words
To make the rivers
  and the birds."

"Hush, my dolly,
 	don't you cry.
We can sing
 	and rock-a-bye.
Kaitlyn's here
 	to care for you"—
All these *important*
 	things to do.

I can color
    pretty trees,
Black and yellow
    bumblebees—
Purple mountains
    standing tall.
Hang my picture
    on the wall.

Set the dishes
    on the table;
Helping hands
    are always able.
Spoons and forks
    and napkins too.
I have *important*
    things to do.

"Lord, it's been
    a busy day.
Time to put
    my toys away."
Working . . . cleaning . . .
    I won't stop!
Fill the toy box
    to the top.

Take off dirty,
   wrinkled clothes.
Scrub my fingers
   and my toes.
See my skin?
   It's just like new.
I have *important*
   things to do.

Drain the water
from the tub.
Bye-bye, bubbles,
glub, glub, glub!
Brush my hair
and dry my face.
Put my toothbrush
in its place.

Pull on jammies,
    warm and snuggly.
Hug my kitty,
    soft and cuddly.
Play a game
    of peekaboo—
All these *important*
    things to do.

Moon and stars
  are shining bright.
Time to rest
  and say good night.
Pray a little
  bedtime prayer:
"Jesus, keep me
  in your care."

If you're big
 or if you're little,
First or last
 or in the middle . . .
You can be a
 helper too.
You have *important*
 things to do.

About the Author

Crystal Bowman received a bachelor of arts degree in elementary education from Calvin College and studied early childhood development at the University of Michigan. A former preschool teacher, she loves writing for young children and is the author of numerous children's books. Crystal is a writer and speaker for MOPS International and has written several books in the recently published MOPS picture-book series.

Besides writing books, Crystal enjoys being active in the local schools, speaking at authors' assemblies, and conducting poetry workshops. Her books of humorous poetry are favorites in the classroom as well as at literacy conferences.

Crystal is also involved in women's ministries, writing Bible study materials for her church and speaking at women's conferences. She has been a guest on many Christian radio programs and has written a book of meditations for moms.

Crystal and her husband live in Grand Rapids, Michigan, and have three grown children.

About the Illustrator

Elena Kucharik, well-known Care Bears artist, has created the Little Blessings characters, which appear in a line of Little Blessings products for young children and their families.

Born in Cleveland, Ohio, Elena received a bachelor of fine arts degree in commercial art at Kent State University. After graduation she worked as a greeting card artist and art director at American Greetings Corporation in Cleveland.

For the past 25 years Elena has been a freelance illustrator. During this time she was the lead artist and developer of Care Bears, as well as a designer and illustrator for major corporations and publishers. For the last 10 years Elena has been focusing her talents on illustrations for children's books.

Elena and her husband live in Madison, Connecticut, and have two grown daughters.

Products in the Little Blessings line

Bible for Little Hearts
Prayers for Little Hearts
Promises for Little Hearts
Lullabies for Little Hearts
Lullabies Cassette

Blessings Everywhere
Rain or Shine
God Makes Nighttime Too
Birthday Blessings
Christmas Blessings
God Loves You
Thank You, God!
ABC's
Count Your Blessings
Blessings Come in Shapes
Many-Colored Blessings

What Is God Like?
Who Is Jesus?
What about Heaven?
Are Angels Real?
What Is Prayer?

I'm Kaitlyn!
I'm Zoë!
I'm Jack!
I'm Parker!

Little Blessings New Testament
   & Psalms

Blessings Every Day
Questions from Little Hearts

God Created Me!
   A memory book of baby's first year